MORE SPECIAL OFFERS
FOR MR MEN AND LITTLE MISS READERS

In every Mr Men and Little Miss book like this one, and now in the Mr Men sticker and activity books, you will find a special token. Collect six tokens and we will send you a gift of your choice.

Choose either a Mr Men or Little Miss poster, or a Mr Men or Little Miss **double sided** full colour bedroom door hanger.

Return this page with six tokens per gift required to
Marketing Dept., MM / LM Gifts, World International Ltd., Deanway Technology Centre, Handforth Road, ...shire SK9 3FB

Your name:_____

Address: _____

_____Postcode: _____

Parent / Guardian Name (Please Print) _____

Please tape a 20p coin to your request to cover part post and package cost

I enclose six tokens per gift, please send me :-

Posters:-	Mr Men Poster	☐	Little Miss Poster	☐
Door Hangers -	Mr Nosey / Muddle	☐	Mr Greedy / Lazy	☐
	Mr Tickle / Grumpy	☐	Mr Slow / Quiet	☐
	Mr Messy / Noisy	☐		
	L Miss Fun / Late		L Miss Helpful / Tidy	☐
	L Miss Busy / Brainy	☐	L Miss Star / Fun	☐

Please Tick Appropriate Box

We may occasionally wish to advise you of other Mr Men gifts.
If you would rather we didn't please tick this box ☐

ENTRANCE FEE SAUSAGES

MR. GREEDY

├─ 100 mm ─┤

250 mm

Collect six of these tokens
You will find one inside every
Mr Men and Little Miss book
which has this special offer.

1
TOKEN

Offer open to residents of UK, Channel Isles and Ireland on....

Join the
MR.MEN & little miss
Club

Treat your child to membership of the popular Mr Men & Little Miss Club and see their delight when they receive a personal letter from Mr Happy and Little Miss Giggles, a club badge with their name on, and a superb Welcome Pack. And imagine how thrilled they'll be to receive a birthday card and Christmas card from the Mr Men and Little Misses!

Take a look at all of the great things in the Welcome Pack, every one of them of superb quality (see box right). If it were on sale in the shops, the Pack alone would cost around £12.00. But a year's membership, including all of the other Club benefits, costs just £8.99 (plus 70p postage) with a 14 day money-back guarantee if you're not delighted.

To enrol your child please send your name, address and telephone number together with your child's full name, date of birth and address (including postcode) and a cheque or postal order for £9.69 (payable to Mr Men & Little Miss Club) to: Mr Happy, Happyland (Dept. WI), PO Box 142, Horsham RH13 5FJ. Or call 01403 242727 to pay by credit card.

The Welcome Pack:

✓ Membership card
✓ Personalized badge
✓ Club members' cassette with Mr Men stories and songs
✓ Copy of Mr Men magazine
✓ Mr Men sticker book
✓ Tiny Mr Men flock figure
✓ Mr Men notebook
✓ Mr Men bendy pen
✓ Mr Men eraser
✓ Mr Men book mark
✓ Mr Men key ring

Plus:

✓ Birthday card
✓ Christmas card
✓ Exclusive offers
✓ Easy way to order Mr Men & Little Miss merchandise

All for just £8·99! (plus 70p postage)

MR. NONSENSE

by Roger Hargreaves

WORLD INTERNATIONAL

Mr Nonsense had no sense at all.

Not a scrap.

I mean, he lived in a tree.

A tree!

Can you imagine?

"Why do you live in a tree?" Mr Happy asked him one day.

"Because," replied Mr Nonsense, "I tried living on the ground, but that was too high up, so I moved to a tree to be nearer the ground."

"What nonsense," snorted Mr Happy.

"Thank you," replied Mr Nonsense.

And, do you know what Mr Nonsense liked to eat?

Porridge!

Nothing wrong with that you might say.

But, porridge on toast!

Really!

"Why do you like porridge on toast?" Mr Nosey asked him one day.

"Because," replied Mr Nonsense, "I tried porridge sandwiches and I didn't like them!"

And, do you know where Mr Nonsense sleeps every night?

In a rowing boat!

In his bedroom.

In his house.

Up a tree.

"Why do you sleep in a rowing boat?" Mr Strong asked him one day.

"Because," replied Mr Nonsense, "I tried sleeping in a motor boat but it was somewhat uncomfortable!"

Mr Nonsense lives, as you might very well expect, in a country called Nonsenseland.

Now, I know somebody else who lives in Nonsenseland.

Do you?

That's right.

Mr Silly!

Mr Silly and Mr Nonsense were close friends and saw a lot of each other.

Mr Nonsense was often round at Mr Silly's house playing jigsaw puzzles.

They used to throw the pieces at each other!

How silly!

And Mr Silly was often round at Mr Nonsense's house playing cards.

They used to tear them up to see who could get the most pieces out of one card!

What nonsense!

However, this story is about the time it snowed in Nonsenseland.

It didn't very often snow, but one winter it did.

Now, tell me, what colour is snow?

No, in Nonsenseland, when it snows, it doesn't snow white snow.

It snows yellow snow!

Don't ask me why.

But it does.

Yellow snow!

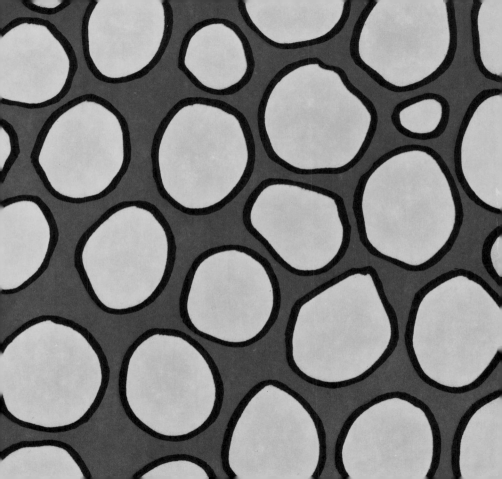

And, when Mr Silly woke up one morning, the whole of Nonsenseland was covered.

"I say," he said when he looked out of his bedroom window. "Snow!"

And he was so excited he rushed round to Mr Nonsense's house.

Mr Nonsense was asleep.

In boat.

"Wake up!" cried Mr Silly. "Wake up, and come and look out of the window."

"What ever on earth is it?" grumbled Mr Nonsense, rubbing the sleep out of his eyes as he got up and went across to his bedroom window.

"I say," he said, looking out. "Custard!"

"That isn't custard, you silly banana," cried Mr Silly. "That's snow!"

He rushed downstairs.

"Come on," he called.

And that day, Mr Silly and Mr Nonsense had one of the very best days of their lives.

They had a snowball fight.

Mr Silly's snowballs were round.

Mr Nonsense made snowballs that somehow or other came out sort of square!

They built a snowman.

A very silly nonsensical sort of a snowman.

"Come on," said Mr Nonsense that afternoon. "Let's go tobogganning!"

"But we don't have a toboggan," said Mr Silly.

"Oh no, we don't," agreed Mr Nonsense.

Mr Silly thought.

"Oh yes, we do," he cried.

And Mr Silly ran back to Mr Nonsense's house, and came back with his bed.

"Wheeeee!" they shouted together as they slid faster and faster down the hill in their rowing boat toboggan.

It was a wonderful day.

And that evening, after having supper together (porridge pie), Mr Nonsense suggested that they played a game.

"What shall we play?" asked Mr Silly.

"Draughts," suggested Mr Nonsense.

"I've forgotten how to play draughts," said Mr Silly.

"Oh, it's easy," replied Mr Nonsense.

And went round and opened all the doors and windows!

"There we are," he said. "Draughts!"

What nonsense!